THE
Little Red Hen

Retold by Michèle Dufresne • Illustrations by Sterling Lamet

PIONEER VALLEY EDUCATIONAL PRESS, INC.

"Please help me,"
said the Little Red Hen.

"No," said the horse.

"Please help me,"
said the Little Red Hen.

"No," said the cat.

"Please help me,"
said the Little Red Hen.

"No," said the pig.

"Please help me,"
said the Little Red Hen.

"No," said the horse.
"No," said the cat.
"No," said the pig.

"Please help me,"
said the Little Red Hen.

"No," said the horse.
"No," said the cat.
"No," said the pig.

"No, no, no!"
said the Little Red Hen.